The Little Cat
and the
Greedy Old Woman

For Judith Garrat

Margaret K. McElderry Books
An imprint of Simon & Schuster Children's Publishing Division
1230 Avenue of the Americas
New York, New York 10020

FIRST UNITED STATES EDITION

First published in London by the Bodley Head Children's Books
Printed in Hong Kong
By arrangement with The Inkman, Cape Town, South Africa
10 9 8 7 6 5 4 3 2 1

Library of Congress Cataloging-in-Publication Data
Rankin, Joan.
The little cat and the greedy old woman : story and pictures / by Joan Rankin. — 1st U.S. ed.
p.   cm.
Summary: A little cat gets his revenge on a greedy old woman who will not share her special meal with him.
ISBN 0-689-50611-2
[1. Cats—Fiction.   2. Greed—Fiction.]   I. Title.
PZ7.R16815Li   1995
[E]—dc20   94-16526

The Little Cat
and the
Greedy Old Woman

story and pictures by Joan Rankin

Margaret K. McElderry Books

One day the greedy old woman got up early.
She started baking and cooking for a very
special dinner. The little cat watched as she
measured and stirred, using all the bowls
and saucepans in the kitchen.

"Mmmm." The old woman licked her lips as she tested each dish.

"Meow," called a tiny voice from under the table.
"I'm getting hungry."
But the old woman paid no attention.

By the end of the day the kitchen was full of delicious smells. The little cat, who had cried out hungrily again and again, could bear it no longer.

He decided to help himself to a teeny tiny taste.

"THIEF!" bellowed the old woman.

Grabbing him by the scruff of his neck,
she threw him out into the rain, and
slammed the door shut.

"Please let me in,"
the little cat cried pitifully.
But no one listened.

So he curled his tail around his wet paws,
closed his eyes, and thought about the warm,
savory-smelling kitchen. He thought about
the old woman who wouldn't share even the
tiniest taste with him.

He felt a very large anger growing inside him.

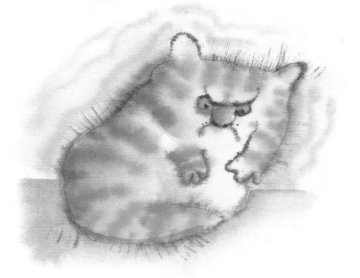

"If only I wasn't so small. If only I could be as large as my anger," wished the cat.

Suddenly, a strange thing happened. The little cat began to SWELL! He grew . . .

BIGGER

and BIGGER.

Soon he was the size of a
GREAT JUNGLE TIGER
and just as ferocious.

He easily pushed through the door
with his heavy weight.

He stamped down the passage to the dining
room, where the old woman was about to
eat the special dinner all by herself.

He growled an angry growl that made all the china rattle.

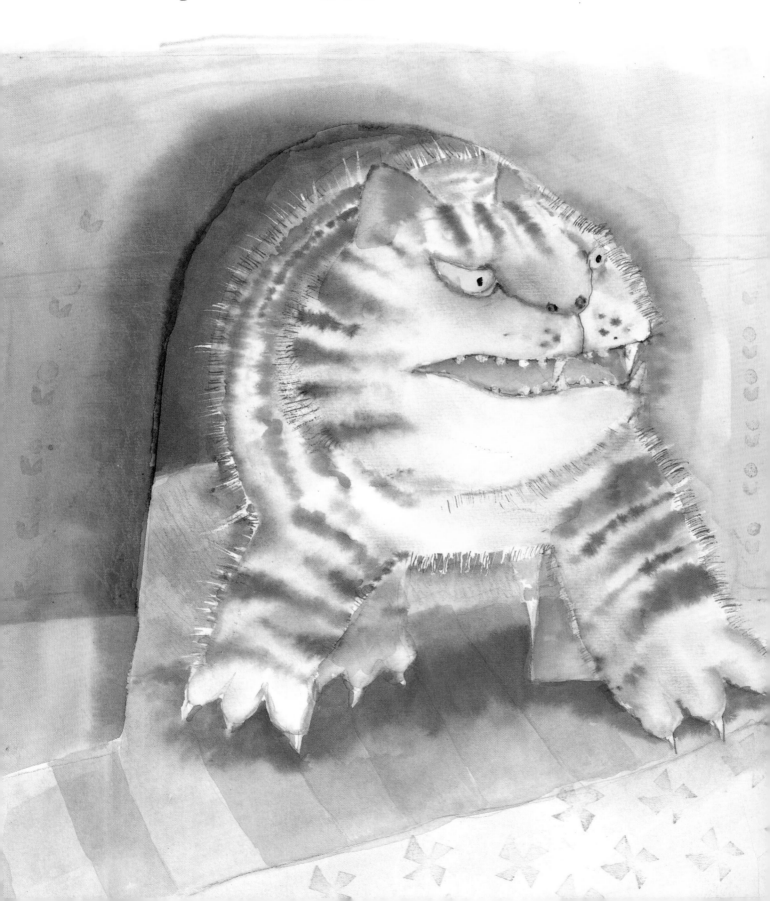

Startled, the old woman looked up, and when she saw the tiger-sized cat she . . .

SCREAMED!

He growled an even angrier growl, and
the furniture shook. In a panic the old
woman scrambled onto the table and
up onto the dining room light.

There she swung trembling with

F E A R .

The giant cat licked his lips. He put his huge paws on the table and began to eat. He crunched the bones with his great teeth and licked the dishes with his enormous tongue until they were shiny clean.

Then he looked up at the terrified
face of the greedy old woman and
smiled . . .

a great wide tiger smile. A great
rumbling tiger purr throbbed
through the room.

He PURRED and PURRED.
And the more he PURRED the more
he SHRANK

until he was just a little cat sitting
on the dining room carpet,
purring a little purrrrrrrr.

At last the greedy old woman
opened her eyes, and when she
saw the *little* cat she stopped
shaking and climbed down from
the dining room light.

She stood next to the little cat
smiling nervously.

Then she went to the kitchen.

She came back with a plate of crackers and cheese.
And she ate them for her dinner. On her soft lap
the little cat slept peacefully.

The old woman was never greedy again.